THE DOOR THAT SHOULDN'T HAVE BEEN THERE

A MODERN FAIRY TALE ABOUT GRIEF

Corinna Edwards-Colledge

WITH ORIGINAL ILLUSTRATIONS BY BECKY GOUGH

CLARET PRESS

Copyright ©Corinna Edwards-Colledge, 2023
The moral right of the author has been asserted.

Copyright ©Becky Gough, 2023
The moral right of the illustrator has been asserted.

Book Cover and Book Interior Design: Petya Tsankova

ISBN hardback: 978-1-910461-67-9
ISBN ebook: 978-1-910461-68-6

All rights reserved. No part of this publication may be reproduced, stored in or introduced into a retrieval system, transmitted, in any form, or by any means (electronic, mechanical, photocopying, recording or otherwise) without the prior written consent of the publisher. Any person who does any unauthorised act in relation to this publication may be liable to criminal prosecution and civil claims for damages.

All characters and events in this book, other than those clearly in the public domain, are fictitious and any resemblance to real persons, living or dead, is purely coincidental.

A CIP catalogue record for this book is available from the British Library.

Printed and bound in Great Britain by TJ Books Limited, Padstow, Cornwall

www.claretpress.com

TABLE OF CONTENTS

PROLOGUE	1
1. THE DOOR INTO THE DARK	9
2. THE DOOR INTO THE MEADOW	19
3. THE DOOR INTO THE WIND	31
4. THE DOOR INTO THE RAIN	49
5. THE DOOR TO THE ROAD	65
6. THE DOOR TO THE SCORCHED FIELDS	81
7. THE DOOR TO THE BRIDGES	99
8. THE DOOR TO THE ICE ISLANDS	115
EPILOGUE	127

This story is dedicated to my father, Paul Edwards, who died in 2002

It is also dedicated to everyone who has lost someone and everyone who one day will.

So, this story is for everyone.

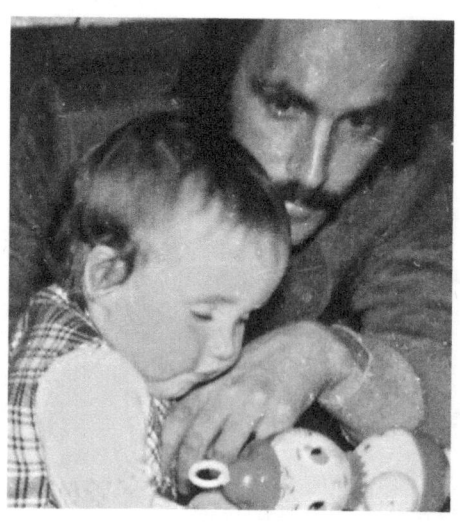

I touch them in the night:
Touch their smooth sealed eyes –
There is nothing whose touch under my fingers
Is so smooth and sorrowful.

Tonight only the breathless pulse of air
And the song of occasional late-birds
Disturbs the space between one figure and another;
I am alone with them and all my memories

(Paul Edwards, Before Sleep, 1957)

PROLOGUE

Once upon a time: that's how all good fairy tales start and it's how this one starts too. But this story also starts with a husband, a wife, and, as you may have already guessed, a Door which comes and goes. I know you must have questions already. But before you have the answers to those questions, you need to know about the wife. About Nella. She is where John's story begins after all.

Come, sit. I shall speak with his voice.

...

I hope everyone loved someone like I loved Nella, or if they're lucky enough to still be young, I hope that one day they will. Even after twenty-five years of marriage I would lie beside her sometimes when she was sleeping with my hand on her arm and think this woman loves me, this woman has chosen to share her life with me. In many ways I couldn't believe it. I'd always thought myself rather ordinary, a bit of a bore even, but the fact she stayed filled me with the most wonderful, deepest sense of contentment imaginable.

When we met, we were both married to other people. It was a terrible mess. There are situations where it is impossible not to hurt someone whichever way you turn, and this was one of them. We tried to minimise the pain but no doubt we made a mess of it. She already had a daughter, Sophie, and amazingly she accepted me. It felt like a gift, a gift I didn't deserve, but there you go. She decided to love me and I loved her back.

When Tom was born it cemented something. We were older then, some would say too old, but we never regretted it. When we got married, he presented us with the rings and Sophie walked her mum down the aisle. My heart felt like it might just burst out of me and fly away like a big white bird that day. It's a cliché I know, but it was the happiest day of my life.

What else to say about Nella? Her favourite colour was yellow and when she wore yellow things they looked so beautiful against her dark skin. I heard David Hockney say in a documentary a couple of years ago: 'The trouble with yellow in a painting is that you never know if it is going to be brighter than white.' It made me think about Nella and the way she glowed in her favourite yellow dress.

The other thing to say about Nella, that partly defined 'Nella' as an entity, as an influence in the lives of others, was her energy. She had the kind of energy that would leave someone breathless. It wasn't that she rushed around all the time; she loved a snuggle on the sofa at the end of the day as much as anyone. It was more a part of her state of being. She was always doing things, she cared about everything, thought about everything. She wasn't just a witness to life, she made things happen and engaged with everything and everyone who came her way.

The other day I was in the loft looking for some old LPs and I noticed for the first time that it was littered with past school projects, the sort found in any family home: a volcano, a Roman shield, a model of the solar system. She was the one who sat down with the kids to make them. She did each one twice. I said to her for God's sake, Nella, just get Sophie's old one out of the loft, no one will know, she went to a different school! But she wouldn't have it. It was fun making it, how could she take that fun away from Tom, that chance to make papier-mâché and mix paint? I apologised. I felt slightly ashamed for my instinct towards laziness, to cutting corners. But she just smiled at me and shook her head.

Nella really saw me, and accepted what she saw. That was her greatest gift to me.

She was hugely affectionate and at the same time she craved affection. I often wonder if I was affectionate enough. I would have tried to give her so much more, but then I suppose I would have been in danger of smothering her.

Nella used to say and, in light of The Door, it came back to haunt me: death is the great leveller. I wonder now if that is true, but one thing I do know is that in Death's eyes, we are all equal. It takes us as we are, without ego and without pride.

1.
THE DOOR INTO THE DARK

Once upon a time a man in late middle age was asleep next to his wife. It was an ordinary night in May, not too hot and not too cold. As usual he was under the duvet, but his wife had thrown it off so that her arms and legs were outside of the covers, her left hand (also as usual) under the pillow beneath her cheek.

And then he woke up, but for no reason that he could fathom. Normally, it would be because of the screeches of foxes romancing at the bottom of the garden; or the noisy return of drunken students heading home from the city centre bars. This time, however, he woke up to silence. He wasn't aware of having been dreaming, he just found himself awake. That was when he first saw The Door.

...

I lay there for a few seconds trying to identify a noise or other cause for why I should have woken. I sighed, turned onto my side and saw on the wall in the gloom over my wife's shoulder a door that shouldn't have been there. There was only a little moonlight in the room, but that was enough for me to see what was plainly in front of my eyes. A door, exactly the same as the door to our bedroom, but on the wrong wall. I turned onto my other side for a moment to see if somehow, inexplicably, the bed had rotated in the night; or if Nella and I had, for some reason that I could now no longer remember, switched sides. But no, the ordinary bedroom door was exactly where it was supposed to be.

So, I turned back onto my left side and the door that shouldn't have been there was most definitely still there. I was about to reach out and give Nella a gentle shake to wake her but something stopped me. My hand retracted, slowly, as if I were withdrawing it from an animal that I was afraid might bite me. Something felt wrong. Of course, a door appearing where before there was no door is most definitely wrong, but it wasn't that. At least it wasn't just that. I told myself to stop being ridiculous and wake up Nella, but at that precise moment she slowly sat up and swung her legs over the side of the bed. She didn't turn or acknowledge me in any way but instead stood up, then steadily made her way towards the door. I tried to shout out, to get her attention, but somehow my voice seemed to have stopped working and my body had lost the power of movement.

Nella's hand reached for the handle and turned it.

The door opened silently. I could see nothing beyond it, just a deep blackness. She stepped over the threshold and I watched her, helplessly, as the pale glow of her nightshirt slowly retreated into the dark. A sense of panic started to overwhelm me and finally I could move again. Grunting with the effort I got out of the bed. My legs felt weak and full of pins and needles, so I shook them and slapped until the feeling came back and I could hasten to The Door. I craned past the open doorway into the space beyond. Nothing felt any different. The temperature was the same as that in my room and, when I gingerly placed one of my feet over the threshold, I seemed to feel only a continuation of the polished floorboards of our bedroom. So, taking a deep breath, I stepped through.

I decided to leave the door open behind me. I had a terrible fear that if it shut I wouldn't be able to find my way back. I called Nella's name but my voice fell back flat as if I was shouting from under a bed or the inside of a cupboard. There was nothing to orientate myself against, only darkness that was at once both solid and permeable. It contained no definition, no edges, no change in shade, and yet there was something about it that seemed to suggest movement in its depths.

I wandered forwards, or at least what I took to be

forwards, looking behind me regularly to check that I could still see the light of the open door. It was still there, but looking at it was disorientating. It created the sense that I was at the bottom of a deep well and, for a moment, I felt like I was falling. I cried out and fell to my knees, catching my breath. A word popped unbidden into my head. A word I hadn't heard for decades, not since studying the Greek underworld at school. Tartarus. The terrifying, bottomless pit of the Gods; the place below the deepest below. The place where they sent the monsters and the traitors for eternities of torment. I think I whimpered then, or some other scared little sound came out of me. Yet the eeriness of my situation convinced me I must be dreaming. I needed to get up and get out of this dream.

I managed to stand a little unsteadily and tried again within the black nothingness to get my bearings. When I looked ahead of me, I cried out, 'Nella!' I could just about see her, a small pale shape somewhere ahead of me. I started to run. It was a strange sensation, as if I was a puppet being put through the motions of running, straining against my strings, only to find I was in fact suspended in mid-air and going nowhere. I shouted in frustration but Nella didn't turn or acknowledge me. It occurred to me that she must be moving faster than I was, though I couldn't work out how. I was exhausted by now and decided to stop and think. I screwed my eyes shut. You can do this, you can find the way out. It's just a dream. You just have to believe you can find the way out.

I opened my eyes again and my heart leapt when I realised that Nella was closer than before. There was another door: a small but distinct grey shape suspended in the centre of my field of vision. It was a welcome sign of normality and definition, like a boat on the horizon line between the night sky and a black sea.

Nella opened the door. I stumbled after her but wasn't able to catch up until she'd gone through it. I reached for the handle.

...

Once upon a time, a man woke up in the morning after a long, troubling dream. The atmosphere of it hung in shreds around him – clingy and disconcerting. It affected him so much he almost felt like crying. He turned over and reached for his wife. But as he wrapped himself around her back, seeking comfort, he found she was cold. At first he was confused. She always throws the duvet off in the night, he thought. She must have caught a chill. He reached down to pull the covers over her but realised that something was not right. She was too still. He touched her again and felt a sense of repulsion. Who put this doll in my bed, he thought in panic. Who has taken my wife and put this doll here? There was something wrong with this shape that looked like his wife. It had the feeling of something that had just emerged from a chrysalis, nascent and still unbreathing. Please let this be an imposter, not her, he thought desperately, but just for a second. He knew this was irrational. The truth was simply this: she was dead.

2.
THE DOOR INTO THE MEADOW

I've always liked the idea of walking at dawn. It's one of those things we think we should do but never get around to, because humans are inherently lazy and the bed is too warm and comfortable. But there is something magical, something other about the dawn; as if our world by dragging itself through the density of the night has been left half transparent, allowing another world to shine through.

That's when I think she went: at dawn.

...

Once upon a time a man watched himself from outside himself. This went on for what felt like weeks but, he found out later, was actually only a few days. His soul was somewhere in the distance, because it had been ripped out of him and couldn't seem to find a way back inside.

The world he now found himself in was a strange one. It was pale and flat, yet, conversely, all the sounds were brash and loud. He felt lost and his sense of existence was tenuous. He knew something terrible had happened. People told him his wife had died but that couldn't be true. He had been with her, just yesterday, she was fine. He heard words like aneurism, didn't suffer and wouldn't have even known…all in her sleep. He tried to absorb these words but couldn't. He remembered a door, and his wife going through it into darkness. He tried to tell the people this, but he couldn't seem to find the words.

Every night, when he climbed numbly into his empty bed, he waited for The Door. But it didn't come – not until he had given up hope of it ever appearing again.

...

I'm ashamed of the person I was that first week. All I can say in my defence is that I just didn't seem capable of being any other way. I barely remember what I did, or who told the children about Nella's death. I now know it was my sister, Anna. Apparently, I called her first. I was hysterical.

Surely everyone has moments from their past which they're ashamed of? The parts they want to forget yet every now and then poke at them in their memory, reliving them until the mouth goes dry and flesh creeps. Why do we do that to ourselves? Maybe it's the price of being a moral being – the need to remind yourself of the depths of selfishness that you are capable of.

My lowest point was when I first properly sat down to talk with Sophie and Tom. Looking back, the narcissism of my mood disgusts me. There is a kind of alchemy between grief and personality; you don't know until it happens how you will respond. Experts may have identified stages that loosely define a shared experience, but in terms of the reality within yourself and your behaviour, everyone is unique. For me, in the early stages, grief stuck to me and bound me tight, strangling my voice and stunting my empathy. Tom and Sophie were reeling. They had just found out that there had to be an autopsy because Nella had died so suddenly. They wanted me to share their shock at this, to comfort and reassure them, but I couldn't. I was there but I was absent, my mind full of self-absorbed, childish thoughts...

> They have it all ahead of them, they are at the beginning,
> I am at the end.
> They have partners and children to hold them,

I have no one to hold me.
They have partners and children to do things with,
I have no one to do things with.
They have careers to occupy them,
I am retired, my life has no meaning.
They have time to heal,
I have no time...
...so little time left, yet now it will feel like eternity.

It was on the fifth night that The Door finally came back. I woke up from a disturbing dream, the details of which ran through my fingers like water as soon as my eyes opened. I lay on my back, heart pounding and the sweat cooling on my forehead. As had happened every time I was dragged nauseously from the world of sleep to find an empty bed beside me, the horror of Nella's death came upon me afresh, crushing me under its merciless weight.

I sat up and hugged my knees, and a strange, shifting light caught my attention and made me turn. This time The Door was ajar, and a warm glow that seemed to tremble and pulse was spilling from it into the room. Adrenaline bloomed in my chest, giving me welcome relief from the unbearable burden of my feelings, and I got out of bed and went towards the light.

This time, the world on the other side of the door was very different: and I found myself looking out at a meadow. Its surface undulated as the wind passed over it in waves. Half of the sky was drenched in a blue so vibrant that it almost hurt to look at it, the other contained a low, bloody sun glowering behind an angry gash of thunderous cloud. The air was hot and oddly charged, and the grasses hissed and shivered.

I contemplated going back for my slippers, but thought better of it. I didn't want to risk the door closing on me, so stepped out into this strange world. The ground was warm beneath my bare feet and as I went forwards, the grasses moved in an oddly conscious way, parting and eddying around me as if helping me pass. I surveyed the horizon. It took a while for my eyes to adjust to the light, but then, I saw Nella and my heart swelled with hope. She was standing beside some kind of monolith, a perfectly rectangular block of dark stone about ten feet high. Something about it tugged at a memory, but I couldn't identify what exactly. This time, instead of her nightgown she was wearing jeans and one of her favourite t-shirts with Salvador Dali's famous lips painting across the chest. I shouted her name until my throat hurt and ran towards her. At first, she didn't seem to hear me, but then, she half-turned, raised her arm and waved briefly.

With a sob of relief, I picked up my pace. I was making good progress, but when I was only fifty yards away she disappeared behind the monolith. Finally, out of breath and sweating, I reached the monolith and ran around it, but to my despair, she wasn't there. I leaned against the stone, defeated and winded, my mind spinning. Something struck me then, the coldness of the stone. Again, the tug of memory. I closed my eyes and searched for it. It came.

I opened my eyes and looked more closely at the monolith. Its surfaces were smooth and about half as deep as it was wide. When I looked upwards from its face towards the sky, it filled my line of vision like a dark, perfectly geometric horizon. It reminded me of the stones that made up the Memorial to the Murdered Jews of Europe in Berlin. Nella and I had visited it only the summer before, in the middle of a northern European heatwave. In thirty-eight-degree heat we had wandered the 200,000 square feet of concrete stelae, their looming shapes creating sharp corridors of alternating blazing sunlight and scalpel-sharp black shadows amidst a mounting sense of unease.

Nella had wandered on, and I'd found myself alone amongst the stones. Despite the incongruous happy shrieks of a group of young Spanish students, I had felt myself descend into a place where the shouts and laughter became tissue thin. I remember laying my hand on the stone in front of me and being shocked to find it cold against my skin, despite the blazing August sunshine. I'd held my breath, feeling a pulse somewhere deep inside the minerals of the monolith, a distant, stony heartbeat of spent horror and loss.

It was the same with this monolith. The surface was cold beneath the blazing sun. I laid my cheek against it and listened for the heartbeat, but there was none. I was about to pull away but then it came to me, a thin echo scratched through the stone – my name. 'Nella! Nella!' I called back. 'Where are you?' But there was no response. I stepped away from the monolith and looked around me desperately. After a few seconds scanning, I saw her ahead of me, the white of her t-shirt flashing through the golds of the shifting grasses. I started after her again.

I'm not sure how long I ran for, but as had happened in the world behind the door on the night of her death, however hard I tried she was always the same distance ahead of me. I started to feel a soreness and itchiness around my calves, and looked down to see that the bottom of my pyjamas were shredded, pinpricked with blood. I stopped, horrified, and pulled them up. My lower legs were crisscrossed with scratches. I looked more closely at the grasses and, tentatively, took one by its length. The edges were like tiny blades and I let go of it with a shudder.

The light suddenly darkened and a rumble of thunder rebounded through the air and into the ground beneath my feet. In desperation I looked about me and saw The Door standing in the grasses, starkly lit by the last rays of the setting sun against a charcoal-coloured storm cloud. As if responding to the thunder, the hissing of the grass intensified and I could have sworn it was deliberately lashing at me. I ran blindly ahead, tears of shock and pain running down my cheeks. It wasn't until I neared the door that the hissing subsided and the grass parted as if willing me to leave.

3.
THE DOOR INTO THE WIND

Once upon a time there was a man and a woman and they loved each other very much. When they met, both were lonely, despite not being alone. They were hungry for touch, but didn't know how hungry until they tasted the sweetness of it. The first night they spent together they went to sleep in each other's arms, and that was how they went to sleep for the next 9,125 nights that they had together.

Sometimes they made love a lot, sometimes they went weeks without it, but whatever happened they always found each other again. The man particularly enjoyed making love in the mornings, sweetly, simply, sleepily, caressing her, letting her lie there, eyes still closed and smiling. The woman told him her favourite was to make love after an evening out, when she was aroused by talking with him and loosened by wine.

They were both getting older now, but they had plans. They talked about exploring new places, building their own home – in a forest somewhere with a magical guest house for the kids and grandkids. Or maybe they would sell up everything and buy a camper van and give the kids their inheritance early. They talked about learning Spanish, or maybe German. Maybe they would take up dancing, it was never too late apparently, or how about giving a home to a couple of rescue dogs? Anything was possible.

But then The Door came, and none of it was possible anymore.

...

When I woke, my pyjama bottoms weren't torn, my legs weren't scratched, and there was no door, except the one that was supposed to be there. I wondered if I was experiencing some kind of psychosis, or particularly lucid dreams brought on by the grief and stress. Sophie had had a spate of terrifying hypnagogic hallucinations not long after Nella and I got together. On one particularly bad night she got into bed between us both telling us she'd seen a witch walk out of her wardrobe carrying a length of rope and laughing at her. The unfathomability of the human mind's ability to torture itself never ceased to amaze me.

Conversely, I accepted The Door on face value. It had appeared, twice, and I had gone through it – to somewhere, somehow, that wasn't in the same world as my bedroom. On a primal level I felt this to be true. I also felt the loss of Nella in this world and the reality of her in the world beyond The Door to be two concurrent but conflicting truths. My consciousness was a battleground between the known and the unknown. Between unbearable pain and the tantalising promises of hope.

On the outside I was doing better. I was able to act the part and get through my days, but it was a disguise. The craftier, self-serving side of my grief wanted people to leave me alone, and I knew this wouldn't happen if they thought I wasn't coping. So, when the results of the autopsy came back and confirmed an aneurysm, I rang a humanist funeral parlour and set the date for the funeral. We were able to bury Nella at last.

'Tom and Sophie are worried about you. I'm worried about you.'

'You don't need to be, Anna. I'm fine.'

'How can you be fine?'

'You're a psychiatrist. Surely if anyone could understand the multiple meanings that can be construed from the word fine, it should be you. Clearly, I am not fine in any way that can be measured in emotional or spiritual wellbeing, but in the English stiff upper lip iteration of the word, I am coping. I am functional. I am surviving.'

'But that stuff you said, when you called me, the night…the night Nella died, you said something about a door. A door that shouldn't have been there. It just made me think that maybe -'

'I was hysterical. Wouldn't you be if you'd woken up and found Peter dead in your bed?'

'I, well, of course, but I-'

'I. Am. Fine.'

'Ok, ok. I just wish you'd let me help with the funeral.'

'I know what she wanted. We'd talked about it. She wanted it to be simple. Non-religious. Natural.'

'Yes, yes, I know, but it feels like you're shutting us out. We all loved Nella you know.'

They all loved Nella. Of course they did. But at that time I held my love for Nella jealously and tight against me. It was mine. I wasn't going to share it. They hadn't spent the last twenty-five years holding her every night, they hadn't learnt to plait her hair, or cooked a special meal for her every Saturday. They hadn't pressed naked against her – felt her thighs and breasts warm on their flesh, her strong arms wrapped around their bare backs. They hadn't comforted her in the middle of the night if she'd had a nightmare. They hadn't fought to be with her against all the odds, even as people turned against you. How could they possibly know what my love for Nella felt like? How dare they even suggest they could.

Even then, I knew in my heart of hearts that this was rubbish. How could I hold my own love for Nella up against the love our children had for her? How could I deny the love of the many friends and colleagues whose lives she had touched and enriched?

...

A bleak wooden house on the top of a hill. You hate the house, but know you don't have the strength to leave it. Everything in the house feels wrong, as if things are slightly out of scale or at a disorientating angle. The corners are deep in shadow; every room is silent and breathless. Outside the windows there is a terrible storm. You look down the hill, the trees are bending their backs to the wind and the sky is a frown of black clouds. You hear a shout, thin against the howling air. There is a path from your front door that runs down the hill. You see shapes at the bottom of it. You recognise them as your friends and family. They are calling to you but you cannot hear what they are saying. There is a huge crash. A tree has fallen across the path in front of them, they shout again and gesticulate towards the house. You bang on the window, you try to call back, but you know there is no chance that they will hear you.

To cut a long story short, John should have been better. John should have been stronger, but was locked in that house, and either didn't know how to get out or simply didn't have the strength.

...

The day of the funeral was a strange, choking sort of day and by the evening I was exhausted. Looking back on it broke my heart, more for them than me, the children I mean. I was strangely detached and competent and read my eulogy without so much as a catch in my voice, and felt a little ashamed by that fact afterwards.

When I got into bed that night I was actually rather drunk. Not your usual raucous, speech-slurring or teary kind of drunk; more the kind of drunk you've steadily, grimly drank yourself into. The type that allows you to kid yourself that you are still sober but feel like you have been hit by a sledgehammer the next day.

I lay there unable to get to sleep, sweating and anxious. Eventually, after an hour or so where I wasn't sure if I had slept or not, a strange sound pulled me into consciousness. It was a slow, steady and regular sound. Thump...thump...thump; like the heartbeat of some immense but distant beast. I lay on my back for a while, staring blankly at the thin stripes of orange and grey that the street light cast through the gaps in the window blind, and tried to establish where it was coming from. I turned my head in the direction I decided was the source of the noise, and there was The Door.

I think I must have still been a little drunk because I got up straight away, much more fearlessly than the previous two times. I leaned against The Door, listening. The sound was louder now, and with each thump of it, the wood of The Door trembled slightly. I took a deep breath, let it out with a hiss through my nose, then took hold of the handle firmly and attempted to pull the door open. At first it wouldn't budge, as if something or someone was pulling at it from the other side. I swore and struggled and finally managed to get it open. A furious howl of wind shot through the gap, sucking at the door and nearly ripping the handle out of my hand. But I was determined to get through and with a grunt I pushed myself against the wind and through the gap. The Door slammed shut behind me.

The cold air that shot through the door was making my eyes water. Although I couldn't see much at first, I had the sense of standing in a vast space. The throbbing sound was deafening now and tangible in the air around me. I wiped my eyes and struggled to focus. I could just about make out the sharp light of stars and realised I was standing under an endless night sky, stark, cloud-free and jewelled. I gasped at the beauty of it then looked around. I was on a large stony plane surrounded by the jagged slopes of ravines, their deepest parts sunk in shadow below me. The wind wasn't cold, but it whipped my thinning hair into my eyes and made balloons of the t-shirt and jogging pants that I had fallen asleep in. I turned around and immediately saw the source of the noise.

On another, higher summit of the mountain I was standing on, was a wind turbine. It stood several hundred feet high, as white and smooth as polished bone, the rhythmic thump of its blades marking a funereal beat in the air. I watched it for a while, mesmerised by its scale and mysterious purpose, then decided I needed to get closer.

I set off, keeping the turbine straight ahead of me. The going was slow, small sharp stones kept sticking into the soles of my feet, and more than once I stubbed my toe on a larger rock that I had failed to spot in the limited light. After a few minutes of walking my eyes were caught by something else. Again, ahead of me, there was Nella, elegantly and seemingly without effort, navigating the rough terrain. This time she shimmered as she moved. That dress, where was it from? Light gold, ankle length and figure-hugging in a simple one-shouldered style. Occasionally she bent to lift the gown when she had to climb, and its folds glinted like molten metal.

'Nella!' Ignoring my sore feet I ran after her. Of course, it was her wedding dress! How could I have forgotten. 'Nella! NELLA!' I called out again, but she didn't turn. I carried on after her.

Our wedding. What a day. It cost a quarter of my first wedding but the atmosphere was light and loving and fun. I didn't mean to be insensitive to my first wife. When we married it had felt like the right thing to do for both of us. Unfortunately, it was too late by the time that it became obvious we were ill-matched; the biggest problem was that I was the only one to admit it. As was often the case, the truth was born with hindsight, and it was the comparison with Nella that proved the truth of this difference. I'd always thought it strange and a little pathetic that, although we spend our whole lives inside ourselves looking out through our own eyes, we didn't believe we could get to the truth of who we were without knowing what others thought about us. But with Nella, that finally made sense. I never knew myself as well as when I started to know myself through her.

Our wedding party went on into the early hours, and it wasn't until the sky started to blush into morning that we finally went to bed and made love. The image and sensation that stayed with me was Nella, naked, astride me. Me in her, her around me, the two of us joined like the answer to an equation:

Nella + Me = $(love)^{(joy)}$

I carried on my pursuit of the golden shape of Nella and still she stayed resolutely ahead, and the colossal turbine kept on its relentless booming beat through the night air...

THUMP

THUMP

THUMP

She disappeared over a ridge and my heart missed a beat. I scrabbled up after her and peered over but she was still there, about two hundred yards ahead of me, scaling a particularly steep ascent that ended with the plane that provided the base for the turbine.

I watched her, my heart in my mouth, filled with a terror that she would slip and I would be forced to watch her slender golden shape tumble into the blackness of the ravine. She hitched up the skirt of her dress and swung her right leg onto the edge of the platform. With seeming ease she then pulled herself onto the flat surface of the summit. She turned and sat on the edge of it, her legs hanging loose, and, for the first time, looked straight at me.

'Nella,' I said again, barely a whisper this time and yet full of longing. 'Oh Nella!'

Filled with newfound optimism I climbed over the ridge and reluctantly turned my back on her so I could more easily descend the other side. I was glad now that I didn't have any shoes on, as I could more easily feel for small ridges and outcrops with my bare toes. I went carefully for a few minutes and was relieved to finally feel the ground beneath the soles of my feet.

I looked up and to my immense relief she was still there. I couldn't tell what her expression was, but the angle of her head and the glint of her eyes told me she was still watching me. I gestured wildly and shouted, then struck forward. As I looked up at the rock face my palms began to sweat. Some sections looked almost sheer and for the first time I was afraid for myself, but I knew there was nothing in this world, or in my own, that would stop me from trying to reach her.

I spent a few moments assessing the climb, spotting a few possible footholds that were just visible by the starlight. To avoid giving time for my anxiety to build I set off purposefully and started to ascend. I tried to keep my momentum going, to trust my body and its instincts to find the safest route. At first it went well, then, about half way up I missed a footing and slid the length of my body down a small natural ramp covered in sharp shingle. The palms of my hands, knees and elbows were scraped raw. I cried out in pain and frustration and looked up for Nella, but there was a small outcrop just above me that cut off my line of sight. The pain and scrapes won't be there in the morning, I told myself. You have to keep going, you have to reach her, to speak to her. How else will you get her back?

Gritting my teeth, I set off again, this time making sure I avoided the treacherous spot that had caused me to slip. At times I thought I didn't have the strength to make it. My arms were shaking so hard and my fingers so numb that when they took hold of the edge of the summit I wasn't sure I would be able to pull myself up and onto it. But then I thought of Nella, of how she was no longer sitting on the edge. I had to know where she was now and that gave me the final ounce of strength I needed to push and drag my body weight up onto the stony platform and the foot of the huge wind turbine.

...

Once upon a time a man stood at the foot of a great windmill. The sky was as black as ink and the stars as white as ice and the blades of the windmill cut through the air with a terrible rhythm. The rhythm scared him but also filled him with yearning, as it reminded him of the beat of his wife's pulse, the beat of the music they would dance to when they got drunk, the inexorable beat of the hours and days they had together. The final beat of her heart that he missed, as he heedlessly slept beside her on that terrible night.

The air was full of the scent of her, of them. He could smell the sweetness of her hair oil on his fingers. He remembered the many nights she asked him to undo the tight plaits in her hair. He remembered the names of the different styles: rope plaits, corn-row plaits, box plaits. Some he had even learned to do for her. The style she had had done for their wedding was so complex it had taken an age to unravel. The realisation that he could never do things for her again, never cook her a nice meal or massage her shoulders after a tough day ached inside him.

He needed her to touch him and tell him everything was going to be ok. He needed to hold her, to speak to her. It felt like a kind of starvation. He searched the bare rock for her but couldn't find her. The windmill relentlessly sliced and set the air humming. At last he saw her, walking around the foot of it towards a small door in its base. Why hadn't he seen it before? She headed to the door and opened it. He called her and called her, he started to sob; he couldn't bear to lose her again, but she didn't seem to hear him and closed the door.

4.
THE DOOR INTO THE RAIN

'Just tell me, Nella, please.'

'Darling, I need a minute. Can you get me a glass of wine?'

I went over to the fridge and poured her a generous glassful then handed it to her. She closed her eyes as she took the first sip and sighed when she puts the glass down.

'Was it Rachel passing her casework onto you again?'

'No.' She sank her face into her hands.

'Did a client have a go at you?'

'It's not that either,' she said in a muffled voice from behind her palms.

I sat beside her and rubbed her back. After a few seconds she leaned against me and started to cry. I put my arm around her and she sobbed gently into my chest. I decided to let her cry it out and not to push her to tell me what's wrong. After a few minutes she disentangled herself from my embrace and wiped her face with a piece of kitchen towel from a roll on the table.

'It's Ralph.'

I felt the air leave my lungs and my chest tightened. *That bastard*, I thought, *I should have known*! She seems to sense the change in my mood. She looks away from me and into the middle distance.

There was so little breath in me that I fought to get each word out. 'What did he do?'

She laid her hand on mine and gave it a squeeze. I took a deep breath.

'He got the Team Manager post.'

'What?' I couldn't believe what I'm hearing. 'How could he, after everything that happened?

'I know.'

'We have to do something. It's not right. How could they reward him like that? It makes no sense!'

'I know, I know, I know!'

I got up from my chair and started pacing about. 'What do we do? Just tell me, Nella, what do we do?'

'I've talked to the union.'

'And?' My tone was hectoring. I made a Herculean effort to soften it. 'What did they say? Can they help?'

'I'm going to take out a grievance.'

'Good. Good! I can help, I can look over the case.' I sat back down, picked up her hand and kissed the palm. She looked up at me. Her eyes were blurry with crying and her mascara had run. I loved her so much at that moment that it felt as if my heart was going to burst.

'Thank you. But it's going to be hard. If I go ahead he

is going to hate me. He could make things very difficult for me. It could look like sour grapes on my part because I didn't get the job.'

'But we have to, don't we? We can't let him, we can't let them get away with it.'

'I know, darling, I know.'

I was not a violent man. I've only had one physical fight in my whole life, but that man, Ralph, I've never hated anyone as much. Nella caught his attention as soon as she joined the team. At first she wasn't sure if she was imagining it, but as time went on and he got bolder, it became unmistakeable. Brushing past her too closely, the odd hand on the knee. The sexualised comments that he passed off as jokes. And then the bits of casual racism, culminating in the day he saw her car, a little Citroen. I'd have thought you'd have a big black Beamer, Nella, he said. Like a drug dealer, he might as well have continued.

So she reported him and he had his knuckles rapped. After that his torments evolved into something new and less easy to prove: undermining her work behind her back, taking her out of email chains, dropping small criticisms about her work in front of colleagues. So, when the team manager role had come up, Nella saw it as a way to fight back, to get a level of authority that would make Ralph back off. After all, like all bullies, he was a coward.

And then he got the job. Nella did take out a grievance and with the help of her union, won. But it was a false dawn. He had the role taken from him but they didn't give it to her either, and the atmosphere became so unpleasant that after six months she felt she had no choice but to move on.

I did something very uncharacteristic the night Nella decided she had to leave the job she loved. Something macho and vengeful. I knew she was going out to commiserate with her favourite work mates, so I waited for her to leave then went into the spare room and dug out one of Tom's old running hoodies. By means fair and foul I had also come into possession of Ralph's home address, and I intended to use it.

Being careful to park the car a good half-mile from Ralph's house in a dark corner where there were no street lights or CCTV cameras, I then traced the route to his rather nice Victorian town house. I kept my hood up at all times and head down. When I got to his house, I posted a well sealed, personally addressed jiffy bag through the letterbox. As an afterthought, and on opportunistically coming across half a brick in the gutter,

I threw it through the windscreen of the brand-new VW Passat estate in the driveway.

I felt lighter as I walked briskly back to my car, partly because I had found a way, however small in comparison to Nella's sufferings, to get some revenge, and partly because of what I had deposited in the jiffy bag.

'You shit in a bag!' Nella was bent over double with laughter, her cheeks varnished with happy tears.

'I did,' I replied proudly.

'Did you...' she was struggling to breathe she was laughing so hard. '...did you shit straight into it, or did you fish it out...' she gulped in air again '...then put it in the bag?'

'I did the shit,' I said sombrely, basking in her hysteria and enjoying playing the straight guy, 'and I looked at it, and I said to myself, this has a purpose, this is destined for great things. And at that moment I knew exactly what that purpose was.'

'What did you use to get it out of the toilet?'

'The barbecue tongs.'

'The barbecue tongs?' Nella repeated, horrified. 'What have you done with them?'

'Washed them and put them back outside, they'll be fine.'

'They will not!' she roared back.

I started to giggle. 'Don't be ridiculous, woman. I fished it out with a rubber glove then threw it away.' The look on her face transformed back into one of joy. She came over, put her arms around my waist and kissed me passionately.

'I love you, husband. I love you for delivering your shit to my tormentor.'

'It is my role, as your lover and champion, to deliver shit to all your enemies.'

'My hero,' she whispered into my ear.

...

Once upon a time a man was lost in memories of his dead wife. She had been buried, he was back at work on a 'phased return', people said how well he was doing, how he was moving on; but he didn't know what moving on meant. Day followed day and night followed night, and still he waited for The Door to return. People came and people went. Friends, family, his children. They drifted through the fog of his consciousness their voices hushed and their arms outstretched for hugs that he returned like a marionette; his arms mechanical and strangely jointed. All he wanted was for The

Door to come and take him to her again. But he couldn't tell anyone about The Door because they might have said it wasn't real, and if it wasn't real then what had he to hope for?

...

By now I was asking myself the very obvious question: *Did any of this really happen?* A door, an actual door that shouldn't have been there, couldn't really have been there...could it be there nonetheless? Things that shouldn't be there simply shouldn't be there: chairs don't float in the sky, cats don't wear hats, fires don't burn in the middle of ice cubes, these things we know, and I agree. My rationality baulks at the notion.

And yet. There it was.

It next appeared about a week after I returned to work. Everyone was worried about me being by myself in the house and their relief was palpable when I decided I would go back. It will do him good they said, take his mind off it. It's not healthy him being shut up in there day in day out. They were right, grief isn't healthy, it isn't healthy at all.

The first week back at work was hard. A lot of people came up to me, their eyes pained, and would pat my arm or even give me hug. *We were so sorry to hear about Nella,* they would say, or *we are sorry for your loss* as if I had accidentally left her at the supermarket. But worse, far worse, were the people who didn't acknowledge her death, who would look away if I walked past them, or leave a room if I entered it. It was as if my association with pain and loss was a communicable disease and they moved around me with a mild sense of fear or disgust. At those moments I would fill with violent urges. I would visualise slamming my coffee cup against the side of their head, or shoving their swivel chair down the stairs with them in it, and it would take every fibre of my being to resist.

The night The Door appeared for the fourth time was the first time I had cried since the terrible morning I found Nella dead. Finding nothing to eat in the fridge, I had investigated the freezer and a frozen portion of Bolognese with Nella's handwriting on it: *spag bol, Nov 19* it said in blue permanent marker on the freezer bag. I had defrosted it, and then eaten it messily through a slurry of tears and mucus. When I'd finished, I'd felt a hot wave of rage take over me and had flung the empty plate against the wall, smashing it into sharp pieces.

Later, exhausted and emptied by tears, I curled up in bed with one of Nella's night shirts clamped against my chest and sank almost immediately into oblivion. It was a dreamless sleep as far as I can remember, and when the patter of rain on my cheeks woke me, the sensation was of being pulled up through dark water.

I opened my eyes and my hand went up to my face. My cheek was damp. I sat up, perplexed, and looked at the ceiling, imagining that there must be a leak in the roof. But it was dry. I went over to the window but the night outside was clear. I turned to go back to bed and that was when I saw it. The Door was there again, flung open, and a mist of fine rain was blowing into the bedroom and settling on the floorboards. At first I felt numb, and then the anger swelled again like nausea. Why was this happening to me? How much more was I supposed to take?

'So you're back are you?' I said, almost with a sneer. 'Not finished with me yet? Well, I'm going to be prepared this time.'

Adrenaline flooding my system, I slid my feet hurriedly into a pair of old trainers. I grabbed my rucksack off the back of the bedroom door (the one that should have been there) and put in a bottle of water and, with a moment of what felt like genius, my mobile phone.

Finally, I put on an old hiking jacket, gritted my teeth and headed through The Door.

The rain was so torrential that for a moment I simply couldn't see the world I had stepped into. The space in front of me was a perpetual shifting plane of grey and an intoxicating scent of damp earth was in the air. The rain hammered against my head and poured over the brow of my hood in a sheet. Within seconds of walking my trainers were sodden and my feet squelched unpleasantly inside them.

The dark column of what I soon realised was a tree trunk came into view, and then another. I appeared to be in a forest, but it was impossible to fathom the time of day because of the downpour. I looked up, squinting against the daggers of rain that were hurtling towards the ground, and saw that the trees were some kind of pine, incredibly tall and straight with black-green crowns. I looked down at my feet and saw I was walking on a thick carpet of needles.

'Nella,' I called out, but my voice was swamped by the hammering noise of the deluge. I walked forward more quickly now and called again, 'Nella!' Still there was no sign of her. I took my phone out of my bag, and, shielding it as best I could from the rain, took some shots of the scene in front of me. I checked the screen and confirmed that the picture had taken. I didn't want the phone to get too wet, so pocketed it again quickly after wiping the screen dry on the part of my trousers that were under the protection of the hiking jacket.

I walked for another five or so minutes, peering into the shifting gloom for a glimpse of Nella. Finally, as I was about to give up and retrace my steps, I saw her. As always, she was a little ahead of me. Her clothes were plastered to her skin by the rain and she was walking slowly, hunched over, hugging her arms around herself as if she was trying to keep warm. I felt suddenly guilty about my fleece-lined jacket and set off after her at a jog.

'Nella, stop, please stop.' I started to take off my coat. 'Here, have my jacket. You're freezing.' However fast I went, and despite the fact that she kept up a modest walking pace, she continued to be resolutely ahead of me. I nearly screamed with frustration: 'For God's sake, Nella, just stop!'

But she didn't stop, she didn't even turn. She kept up her nonchalant pace while I tried to run after her, slithering and sliding in the soaking earth. I stopped for a moment, catching my breath. The rain was pouring off my hood and into my eyes. I wiped at them furiously.

'Why won't you stop? What do you want from me?'

She paused momentarily at that and turned to look at me. The gesture spurred me on, and I scrambled to my feet and set off again thinking that this time I might catch her. But after just a few yards I slipped and fell face first into the mud. I beat my hands wetly against it and howled with rage.

Eventually I pulled myself together and managed to scramble to my feet. There was no sign of Nella, but The Door was there, waiting for me.

5. THE DOOR TO THE ROAD

'What does it look like to you?'

Tom squinted at my mobile screen then turned it 90 degrees and squinted at it again. 'Something green. It's a bit blurry, Dad.'

'It's forest, can't you see?'

'Hmm.'

Sophie came over and took the phone from Tom. 'Yes, I can see that I think, the dark straight bits are tree trunks. But you've got to remember to press on the screen where you want to focus. I keep telling you.'

'It was raining,' I replied, a little more petulantly than I meant to.

She sat down beside me and laid her hand briefly on mine. 'Where did you take it?'

'I recognise that jumper,' I said, to change the subject.

Sophie pressed the sleeve of the jumper to her nose. 'It's Mum's favourite. The one she'd wear when she wanted to chill out at the end of the day. It smells of her.'

She held her arm under my nose and I flinched slightly. Pulling myself together I held it closer. A soft echo of familiar perfume made the fibres of my soul ache. 'Yes, it does.'

Sophie sniffed and wiped at her eyes. She looked exhausted and drawn. 'I still can't believe it,' she said in a whisper, 'How is it possible? She was in this jumper just a few months ago, living and breathing and laughing. It just doesn't make sense.'

Tom stopped for a moment in his transference of a pile of Nella's clothes into a charity clothes bag and I noticed his hand was shaking. I knew I should say something but couldn't for the life of me think what.

'We've had a terrible shock,' I finally managed to blurt out, and the peculiarity of the statement made me want to punch myself in the face. 'We've got to stick together,' I continued with another unnecessary platitude, compounding my self-loathing.

'But we aren't, are we?' Sophie said quietly.

'Of course we are!'

'It's like you've been somewhere else, Dad.' Tom added, looking at me sideways for a second, then looking away again, blushing.

'I don't know what you mean,' my voice emerged from my tightening chest, squeaky and defensive. 'I've been here every day.'

'We're not saying you haven't been here, as in this

location,' Sophie continued for Tom, 'but that you haven't been present, as in with us.'

'Well for God's sake, Sophie, what do you expect from me? I've gone back to work, I've agreed to go through her things, I'm trying to move on as everyone keeps saying I need to do. I'm dealing with this in my own way as I'm sure you are too.'

Sophie quickly wiped away a tear and my heart ached for her, but my arms stayed heavy by my side.

'We just didn't expect to be grieving alone, that's all.'

That evening was a red one. I was filled with indiscriminate fury greater than I had experienced since Nella died, and everything that happened to me compounded it. I broke one of my favourite wine glasses; I got a Tupperware lid stuck in a kitchen drawer so I couldn't open it; I stood in fox shit when I went to put the bin bag out bare-foot.

As I insisted on avoiding the truth that I was really angry with myself rather than anything else, I remained trapped in the whirlwind of my own temper. After then accidentally trapping my finger in the bathroom door, I howled and crashed about like a wounded bear. I shouted expletives, to the universe, to Nella, to God, I stamped around the house, alternately crying and shouting. I'm amazed the neighbours didn't call the police; I can only assume they were on holiday.

Finally, feeling sheepish and drained by my outbursts, I dragged myself up to bed without even stopping to brush my teeth. To my shock, The Door was there. No falling asleep this time, no question that I may be dreaming.

It was.

Simply.

There.

It was closed, but there was a low rumble coming from the other side of it, like the sound of an engine. I was afraid this time. I felt exposed and vulnerable. It wasn't supposed to happen like this, so boldly and viscerally. It was supposed to sneak up like a dream in the night, retaining a sense of mystery.

After a few seconds of indecision, I realised that my need far outweighed my fear, and went to The Door. My hand hovered over the handle for several seconds. My nerves, I realised, were shot by seeing the kids and going through Nella's clothes. I gulped, pushed my shoulders back, gripped the handle hard and pulled.

This time there was no meadow, mountain or forest. This time I found myself in a plain, rather dingy garage lit only by a single bare bulb. A large, expensive-looking black car was idling. The shocking mundanity of these new surroundings made me gawp with incomprehension. Eventually, the driver's door opened and a tall, thin man got out. His chauffeur's hat was pulled so far down that the stark glare of the bulb overhead cast his whole face in shadow.

He walked up to the passenger door and opened it. I wanted to speak but nothing would come out. With a single, oddly jerky movement, the Chauffeur gestured towards the open door with a black-gloved hand. Every ounce of being was screaming at me to turn back and into the safety of my bedroom, but I didn't. I remembered all those times that Nella would shout at the TV, berating some fool for getting into a car with the local Mafia boss only to be driven to the woods and forced to dig his own grave. Yet here I was, repeating their mistake.

The Chauffeur slammed the passenger door shut and climbed back into the driving seat. He put the car into gear and immediately the garage door opened and he drove out.

'Where are we going?' I asked stupidly.

The Chauffeur didn't answer. I saw that there was a glass partition between us. The car was old and luxurious, with walnut trim, leather seats and a small red velvet curtain that framed the glass that separated me from the front seats.

'Have you seen Nella?' The driver turned at that, but not to me, to the front passenger seat. My heart jumped into my throat. 'Nella?' I reached forward and pulled back the curtain and there she was, just two feet away from me.

'Nella!' I banged on the glass between us but she didn't turn. 'Nella, why won't you look at me? You must be able to hear me!' The more I banged on the glass the angrier I got. But neither the driver nor Nella turned or acknowledged me in any way, and the big black limousine continued on its smooth journey, engine purring.

Almost beside myself with frustration, I looked out of the window and saw we were on a long, straight road through a flat and featureless landscape. The sky was still dark at its crown but lightening at the horizon line. I had an idea. I shifted across the back seat until I was sat directly behind Nella. I tried the button for the electric window, and with a huge sense of relief watched it slowly, soundlessly descend.

For a moment the rush of air from outside distracted me. It was cold and iron-rich, leaving a faint taste of blood in my mouth. I grimaced with distaste but leaned out of the open window so I could bang on the glass of the front passenger door.

'Nella, please look at me. Why won't you look at me?'

I could only see the side of her head and she didn't turn. The wind rushed past me, pulling my skin tight against my skull, and the road slid queasily below me.

'Nella, for God's sake…not again!'

I felt a wave of exhaustion sweep me. I was so tired of being angry.

Her hands moved in her lap and I saw she was holding something in her hands. I propped myself further out of the window, as far as I dared, and saw it was a photo of Tom and Sophie. It was her favourite picture of them, taken at a local open farm. Little Tom was sitting on an old broken tractor pretending to drive, and Sophie was perched on the bonnet, smiling at a big red hen that had jumped up beside her.

The sight of the children winded me and I dropped back into my seat.

All I could remember was how they'd looked at me this evening, red-eyed and anxious. Was I letting them down? The question had a ruthless velocity to it which made me close my window and sink into shame-filled introspection. Had I been selfish in my grief? I had thought of nothing but her since she died. Every second, waking and dreaming, had been filled with her. I rather felt that I had no choice in the matter. But in so doing I had failed in the one area she would have most wanted me to be strong in: supporting my children.

The car growled to a stop, distracting me from my thoughts. I looked up and saw that we were at some kind of toll booth. A wooden arch with thick beams of wood, damp and scabbed with patches of dark green moss, stood over the road. I opened the window again. The air was brackish now and, as my eyes focused, I saw that the road had come to a stop at the bank of a broad, fast-flowing river.

I shifted back to my spot behind the Chauffeur. From this side, I saw that he had opened his window and seemed to be in discussion with a dark figure who had come out of the booth and stooped down towards him. The driver then turned to Nella and held out his hand. I watched them, rapt and strangely anxious. Nella took the photo of the children and passed it to the driver. He, in his turn, carefully and reverentially passed it to the dark figure at the door. I strained to look at what the figure did with the photo but he had his back to me.

The crooked, hollow sound of a bell resonated through the air and then the car started to move again. We seemed now to be, impossibly, floating across the water. I opened the window and peered down and saw that we were, in fact, on a small wooden jetty or raft which was being pulled by a stout rope that must have been fixed on the other bank. The water showed signs of a strong current and I could hear the *slap slap slap* of it against the sides of the raft, but our passage across felt more like hovering.

After a few minutes I could see the other side of the river, a frill of dark earth against the luminous grey. Dawn had broken now and a pale sun was slowly rising over the horizon line.

I felt a wrenching tilt in my centre of gravity, tearing at somewhere near my heart.

'Nella.' I sat forward and pressed my palm against the glass panel between us. 'I'm sorry, I'm so sorry. I've let you down, I've let the kids down, I see that now. I will make it up to them, I promise.'

She sat there with her back to me, each moment spinning out a new thread of agony.

'It suited me to believe that if I didn't let them see it, I was protecting them, but that was just a lie I told myself. What I was really doing was not letting their pain through me. I thought it would be unbearable. I'm sorry, Nella.'

I waited.

I breathed.

I felt the heat of my hand warm the glass.

And then she turned.

And she looked at me.

'Oh Nella!' The tears ran down my face. She held my gaze, her eyes steady and free of reproach. Her expression was still, her mouth neither smiling nor downturned; but somehow, it was full of meaning. She still knew me and accepted me. My heart beat faster, and my throat tightened. I knew I had to leave her for our children's sake, but not here, not now. There was so much more I wanted to say, that I needed to say.

The car came to a stop. Nella broke the thread of our connection and turned back to look ahead. I hammered at the glass, desperate to keep her attention, even for just a second more.

'Darling, no, please stay, please!'

My door opened, the Chauffeur standing behind it. I looked out and saw we were in another garage, similar to but not exactly like the one I had left. For a moment I considered remonstrating with him, or going up to Nella's door and trying to open it. But I remembered my pledge to her and all the fight fell out of me. I understood, at least in part.

I stepped out of the car. 'Thank you,' I managed to

murmur to the driver, who gave the briefest of nods, his face still drowned in the shadow of his peaked cap.

Summoning every atom of my willpower I walked towards The Door, which of course was exactly where I knew it would be. I didn't try to look back, though every part of me was screaming to do so. Instead, I counted. It took six short steps to get to The Door. I reached out and took hold of the handle. It felt familiar now, though I couldn't work out if I loved or loathed it.

I heard the engine of the car start.

Don't look back.

Don't look back.

It started to reverse.

Don't look back.

Don't look back.

I let out a long, shuddering breath, opened The Door, and walked through it.

6.
THE DOOR TO THE SCORCHED FIELDS

'So, Granddad – are you listening, Granddad?'

'Hm? Sorry...yes.' I pushed Ella on the swing again and felt the bracing muscles of her back against my palm.

'So, when the cats see the zombies their eyes light up because they have special powers but they only have the special powers at night and in the daytime they're just like normal cats and their claws have a special poison in them which makes the zombies die –'

'Aren't zombies already dead?'

'This makes them proper die, like they can't move or eat anyone anymore and you can tell the special cats because their whiskers are zigzagged like lightning and when the zombies are all dead the cats go and tell their owners that it's safe to come out now so all the owners come out of their hiding places and have a big party.'

'I think it sounds like a wonderful story. You should definitely write it down.'

'Mummy's teaching me to type in a special way where you don't look at your hands and it's like there's eyes in your fingers and they know where the letters are.'

'You mean touch typing?'

'Yes, touch typing. Mummy's really good at it.'

Sophie appeared at the back door. 'Time for lunch now you guys.'

I slowed the swing and went around to the front to help Ella down.

'Mummy no, five more minutes, I want to do rockets!'

'Ok, sweets, but then come in before your food gets cold.'

Ella's eyes narrowed at the word cold. 'What is it?' she asked warily.

'Soup.'

Ella pulled a face. 'I hate soup.'

Sophie came over and ruffled her daughter's hair. 'Don't be ridiculous, you don't even know what kind of soup it is!'

'Soup is soupy. It'll have bits in. Your soup always has bits in.'

Sophie put her hand on my shoulder and rolled her eyes. I looked down and lightly kissed her forehead. She smiled at me. 'Anyway, be inside in five minutes.'

Ella watched her mum go back to the house with a look of proprietorial content then turned back to me. 'Rockets, Granddad!'

'If Princess –'

'Queen,' she corrected me.

'If Queen Ella commands rockets she shall have rockets!' I took hold of her ankles and pulled her up to shoulder height and she squealed with delight. 'Three… two…one…blast off!' I let go of her ankles and she shot backwards and straight up the other side.

'Again! Again!'

'Ok, one more time -'

'Three more times!'

'Two more times, then it's in for lunch.'

We did rockets two more times. I got her up as high as I could without pulling a muscle. Afterwards, as she settled back to a gentle rocking, I noticed her shoelace was undone and knelt down to tie it. As I straightened up, with my customary groan, she took hold of my face between her small hot hands and stared straight into my eyes.

'I still feel Nanna Nella.'

I covered her hands with mine. 'Me too.'

Her gaze was clear and I felt it pierce my heart somewhere small and tender. I thought about the world she was growing up in: its inept, psychopathic leaders, its burning forests and melting glaciers, its tribalism and inability to learn the lessons of history. I thought about the species of plants and animals that we would never see again, the islands of plastic blooming on the oceans like tumours, and all at once I felt a crushing sense of shame and powerlessness. But it wasn't just that, I reflected, I also sensed an overwhelming need to be able to hope. To hope that she wouldn't have to grow up in a world where the nihilistic greed of a few billionaires had stolen her dreams and her safety. That nature would it somehow, prevail. My heart burst open like a flower, exposing something raw and painful inside. Ella pulled a hand away and pointed a finger gently to my cheek. It came back with a tear on it.

'Don't worry, Granddad. I'm sure the soup won't be that bad.'

...

Once upon a time, actually about seven years ago, there was a man, sitting in the kitchen of his step-daughter's house, waiting for his first grandchild to be born. He didn't know how long he had been there. Every now and then his son-in-law or the midwife or Nella would come downstairs to get his step-daughter a bit of food or a hot water bottle and give him progress reports. At some point his son joined him and they chatted in hushed voices, the animal cries of the birthing mother flying fiercely through the house.

They made spaghetti with garlic, chilli and parmesan. His son's favourite comfort dish – a panacea over the fifteen years of his life for everything from illness and exam stress to being bullied. The dog kept pacing about and whining, as if picking up the energy waves of his step-daughter's labour.

More hours went by. The man's son fell asleep on the sofa and he, with his head on his arms on the kitchen table. Eventually he felt a hand on his shoulder, it was the midwife. His grandchild had been born. He woke his son and they trod, reverentially, up the stairs. The mother was in bed her face shiny with exhaustion and happiness. The baby was curled up in the crook of her arm like a flower, its eyes tightly shut. By the bed, stroking her daughter's arm, was Nella. She looked up at him. They're calling her Ella, she said, isn't that wonderful. He felt the hairs rise on his arms and he shivered. At that moment she looked like a goddess to him all ablaze, with love sparking in her eyes.

...

I stayed at Sophie's that evening. Ella wanted me to read her a bedtime story, and it was good to catch up with Sophie's husband, Sam, who I hadn't seen for a long time. We had a roast dinner, then watched a Harry Potter film. Ella had her bath, then cajoled and inveigled a total of four stories from me. When I finally left her, I was exhausted, so soon after made my excuses to Sam and Sophie and headed up to bed in the spare room.

I hadn't seen The Door for weeks and the reality of it was at a low ebb. At those moments I tried to convince myself that it was just a case of temporary grief-provoked psychosis. Even the forest picture on my phone lost its power; it was just a pocket photo, my rationality argued. So, when I walked into Sophie's spare room and saw The Door there on the far wall, I actually went back out into the hall, closed the door (the one that should have been there), opened it again, looked round and saw that The Door hadn't budged.

Heart beating hard I went downstairs and into the living room where Sophie and Sam were watching the news.

'Sophie.'

She looked round distractedly. 'Yes?'

'Could you just come upstairs for a minute, I'm not sure that I've got the right bedding out of the cupboard.'

'Oh, ok.' She swung her legs off the sofa and followed me upstairs. When she walked into the room my eyes kept flicking to The Door (that was still very much there), then back at her.

'Have you redecorated in here or something?'

She looked at me and frowned. 'No, it's just the same.'

'Oh.'

It was obvious that she couldn't see The Door.

She went over to the bed. 'Yep, that's the right bedding. Goodnight.'

We hugged, but as she pulled away she looked at me with concern. Her spontaneous affection had turned on the waterworks again.

'Don't worry, I'm crying a lot these days.'

She smiled and gently cupped my cheek with her hand, just as Ella had done earlier, then she went back downstairs and I was left, just me and The Door, my mind racing.

I closed the normal door and paced for a moment. It would be impossible to sleep, to pretend it wasn't there, that much was obvious. There was no point feigning illness and heading home as I'd had a few glasses of wine so couldn't drive, and anyway, who was to say that The Door wouldn't be waiting for me when I got there? As usual, despite my better judgement, despite my misgivings, despite my existential crisis about whether it was there at all, the truth remained that if

The Door appeared, I was beholden to go through it. Like Chekhov's gun that must be fired.

I went over to The Door and placed my hand on it. It felt warm. I pressed my nose against the tiny gap between The Door and the frame, and breathed in. Was it my imagination or was there a faint smell of burning? I walked away and back again, three times. Finally, I opened the door and went through it.

My first reaction was terror, and I very nearly turned volte-face back through The Door.

The sky was filled with fire.

It licked and swirled and boiled, miles above my head. Smoke gathered like rain clouds and the ground beneath my feet was blasted and burned.

What kept me there, what stopped me turning heel and fleeing this new hellish world were three things. Firstly, it was hot, Spain in August hot, but not unbearably so. Secondly, despite the incendiary drama of the sky, the air seemed clear and my breathing was unlaboured. Thirdly, I was standing on a path. A strip of earth, slightly more compacted than the rest, which traced a straight line from my feet to the horizon.

I set off down the path, my eyes constantly drawn to the ever-shifting drama of the sky – much as your eyes are drawn to an open fire in a darkened room. The regular padding of my feet, the monotony of the landscape and the sinuous flicker in the air above me made the process of walking strangely hypnotic. I lost all track of time. I could have walked for hours and I felt strangely calm.

Then I saw the first bird. It was on its back, a few metres in front of me, its wings flapping feebly. I went up to it, a combined sense of pity and revulsion making my skin prickle. I crouched down and looked more closely. Its feathers were singed and its eyes appeared to have been burned shut. My hand went to my mouth, but a grunt of horror still escaped. What could I do, here, to help it?

Like a film starting up in a dark cinema, my mind started to play a long-lost memory of walking with my father in Hyde Park, on one of my rare weekends back from school. It was a breezy day in May and we came across a nest that had been blown out of a tree by the previous night's gale. There was a chick inside the nest, a tiny thing made of pink trembling flesh, so young its eyes were still tightly closed. Its beak opened and shut pathetically, and it appeared to be stuck on its side as if its back had been broken.

I was about to suggest that we pick the chick up

and take it home. Our Head of Year had raised a crow chick that he had found and we had taken turns feeding it through the night for the first few weeks. By the time it had grown to adulthood it was completely tame and would sit happily on people's shoulders and peck at their ears. We loved that bird.

Before I had a chance to speak, however, my father placed his brown-brogued foot over the chick and pressed down hard. I think I screamed, and my father looked around sharply with a frown. Whatever's the matter? he asked me, as if he'd done something as innocent as buttering a piece of bread or turning on the television. You know I've done it a kindness, he continued, wiping the sole of his shoe on the grass, it would have starved to death down there or been savaged by a cat. On some level I knew he was probably right, on the other, the act felt irrevocably cruel.

I felt nauseous as I turned back to the bird. It was clearly suffering. As I accepted the truth of what I must do, the horror of it rose simultaneously like bile in my throat.

'I'm sorry. I don't know what else to do.' I placed my foot over the bird's head and stamped down. The fragility of its skull shocked me, I barely felt it break. I knew I couldn't bear to look at what was beneath my shoe, but the bird's wings had stopped jerking so I looked resolutely ahead of me and walked away, dragging my right foot slightly on the dirt of the track to clean it.

I felt like I had come through some terrible but singular event, but I was wrong. As I continued to walk, there were more scorched birds strewn across the path. Most were dead, or at least unmoving, but occasionally I found one that was still alive. One had had a wing scorched off so that only the thin fan of bones remained, another had stumps where its legs should have been. Each time I took a deep breath and stamped on the bird's head, each time I felt a lurch of disgust and shame in the pit of my stomach. It was relentless; I could feel my nerves shredding. After I had killed about two dozen birds I broke down. I curled up on the ground, sobbing and holding my knees to my chest. I cried like I hadn't cried since I was a child. Unrelentingly, utterly, my eyes and nose running into one oleaginous mess of sorrow. I cried until there was nothing left.

Exhausted, I rolled onto my back and was surprised to see that the fire in the sky was thinning and being replaced by a delicate blue. I dragged myself back to standing and looked about me. The birds had disappeared, a shimmering mass of green lying ahead.

My heart thudding with hope, I ran for what felt

like miles, never tiring or struggling, a youthful energy flowing up through my legs through my chest and up to my scalp. As I got closer, the green revealed itself to be a small oasis, fringed with willow trees and ferns. I stopped at its edge, pushing through to find a small but beautiful pool of clear water. I felt hot and sticky, and the sight of the water was irresistible. I started to undress.

As I peeled off my underpants and went to the edge of the water, a series of ripples started out from the centre, and after a few seconds Nella burst through the skin of the pool. She was naked too, and the water ran down her neck and shoulders like mercury.

'Nella!'

She smiled at me and dived neatly back down into the pool. Without a second thought, I ran and leaped into the water, feeling its cool kiss over my body. The pool seemed extraordinarily deep for its size, and I could see the silver paths of tiny fish crisscrossing beneath me. I swam back to the surface, took a deep breath, then dived again. I could see Nella now, as ever, a little ahead of me, swimming deeper and deeper. I knew if I went up for air I'd lose her. Repressing every instinct to the contrary, I swam after her.

My arms carved arcs through the water ahead of

me, and my legs beat time with my stroke as I swam, furiously, after Nella's retreating figure. Then, just as I drew near to her, Nella turned back and beckoned to me. She wanted me to follow her. There was no mistaking it. But in that same moment of excitement, I suddenly realised that I was desperate to breathe. The muscles of my chest screamed for release and a sense of panic was threatening to overwhelm me. I looked up. The surface of the water seemed an impossible distance away. I looked back down. The Door was there, just below me.

Waves of agonising pain grabbed at my lungs. I couldn't see Nella. Was she somewhere in the depths below me or had she gone through the door? No longer able to control my instincts, I inhaled involuntarily and choked on the water. I could feel myself slipping away. With a wrenching effort, I swam desperately towards The Door. As my hand touched the handle everything went black.

My bulk hit the floorboards with a thud, naked and soaking wet. I lay there, gasping up water. Shaking, I finally got up, snagged a towel from the back of a chair and wrapped it around my waist. With a convulsive shudder I realised I'd nearly died. Had I meant to? The thought was chilling and I felt tears well up in my eyes, but I was unsure who they were for. I looked at the clock on the bedside table. 7.30am. Thin sunlight was leaking through the gaps in the curtains.

Why was I wet? When I'd been through the door before, whatever I'd experienced had been left behind in that other world. But then there was the photo, and now this. Perhaps the longer I spent on the other side of the door, the more its influence passed back with me. I shuddered.

'How did you do that, Granddad?'

I turned with a start. Ella was standing in the doorway, silhouetted against the morning brightness of the hall. My tears, I realised, were for her.

'Do what, sweetheart?' I managed to choke out the words.

'How did you make that door disappear?'

7. THE DOOR TO THE BRIDGES

Once upon a time a man was at a conference and he was bored. It was a conference about something he was only mildly interested in, in a town that he would instantly forget the minute he left it.

It was his first time away from home in a couple of years and he was finding the opportunity for reflection both a blessing and a curse. The big question was, did he have the courage or honesty to listen to what his inner voice was telling him, in those long hours alone in his hotel room at the end of each day?

The speaker was now expounding on the virtues of infographics, and how they helped disseminate information in an easily digestible and inclusive way, when the man felt his gaze start to drift. He scanned the circular tables of delegates arranged across the room in front of him until his eyes came to an abrupt stop.

A striking woman, the only black woman in the room as far as he could see, was half turned in her seat and staring straight at him. It wasn't an aggressive or challenging look but it was steady and appraising. Her eyes were bright with intelligence and he could see the beginnings of a smile soften her face. He felt his heartbeat quicken.

Don't look like an idiot, he whispered internally, and struggled to maintain his composure and smile at her. To his delight, she smiled back before turning around in her chair to face the speaker again.

At the end of the session, when getting a coffee from the refreshment table, he was both shocked and thrilled when the woman tapped him on the shoulder. You know you fell asleep for five minutes during that talk, she said. Maybe they should produce an infographic on how to stay awake during boring conferences, he had replied, pleased with himself for finding a modicum of off-the-cuff wit to deliver back to this beautiful woman. I pinch the back of my hand when I get sleepy, she replied, but the worst thing you can do, she continued, is actually close your eyes, even for a split second, then you're fucked. It's downhill from there. He snorted into his coffee cup when she said that, but she didn't seem to mind. In fact she threw back her head and laughed, and her voice boomed around the room so loudly that everyone in the refreshment queue turned to look at her. He wondered if that happened to her a lot, and how often she was the only black woman in a room full of white men in suits.

Some people think it only happens in fairy stories, but they're wrong. This could happen to anyone at any moment, this sense of connection, of inevitability, when someone meets another being with whom they know they have to be.

...

The counsellor had a large, shiny red face, as if his head had been blown up through his shirt collar like a balloon. For the first ten minutes of the 'therapeutic hour' this image obsessed me, but I soon realised that the counsellor was a person of intelligence and profound focus, and I felt ashamed at the superficiality of my initial assessment.

'What's going through your mind right now?'

I blushed. 'I was thinking...' I stammered out, 'of the day I first met Nella.'

'Would you like to tell me about it?'

'It was at a conference, I can't even remember what it was about now, but I was thinking of how by the end of that first day, we knew that we were going to be together.'

'How did you know that?'

'It's hard to explain. Our being together meant making a terrible mess, of other people's hearts – spouses, children, in-laws – but despite that, our being together was inevitable. We were both profoundly lonely, you see. People forget that you can be more alone with the wrong person than by yourself.'

'So, when you were with Nella, you never felt lonely?'

'No, never. If anything, what I felt with her was the opposite of loneliness, whatever that is.' I felt a sob thicken at the back of my throat and struggled to keep it down. 'Of course,' I continued, hoarsely, 'it's not that it was always perfect, but we were always together, even when we disagreed, even if we had let each other down, we were always able to get back. Somehow, we were never truly apart, even when we were – practically and geographically – if you know what I mean.'

The counsellor nodded. 'And now?'

'I'm sorry?'

'Do you feel truly apart now?'

'I...' His question floored me for a moment, as if he somehow knew about The Door. For a crazy second I even considered telling him about it. 'In some ways it feels like she's still here,' I replied carefully, 'in other ways it feels like her apartness is so absolute and terrible it's as if I've lost a limb.'

The counsellor crossed his legs and looked at me. 'Would you say you are a different person for knowing her?'

'Undoubtedly, irrevocably.'

'Has it changed how you communicate? What you care about? How you parent your children?'

'Yes, all of those, everything.'

'Then in a way she will always be here, and her essence passes through you in every interaction you make, in every relationship you cherish.'

I absorbed his words and nodded. The tears rolled heavily down my cheeks and onto my clasped hands. I wanted to say thank you to him but I couldn't speak.

My first session with the grief counsellor left me exhausted. I felt wrung out and battered, like the favourite teddy bear of a loving but heedless toddler that had been dragged around by its ear all day. Conversely, there was also a welcome feeling of calm and stillness; something I hadn't felt for a long time.

After a quick dinner I poured a brandy and went out to sit in the garden. Although it was mild, the evenings were drawing in and the edges of the garden had started to melt into darkness. I sat on the old wrought iron bench (which I noticed was in dire need of a new coat of paint) and took a deep gulp from my drink.

I closed my eyes. A lone blackbird was singing plaintively somewhere in a neighbour's garden and the hum of distant traffic hushed and whooshed like breathing. Keeping my eyes closed I took another slug from the brandy and followed its warm journey down my throat and into the centre of me. I felt at peace in a way I hadn't in a very long time.

Something rubbed against my leg and I opened my eyes with a start. I looked down to see a large black and white cat staring back at me. It hrrupped in a friendly way and I rubbed its head. I felt for a collar but there wasn't one.

'Where have you come from then, eh?'

The cat purred and slinked around my ankles, then trotted off across the lawn. I gazed after it then nearly dropped my glass when I watched it slip through The Door, which had appeared amongst the shadowy tangle of the laurels at the bottom of the garden.

'What are you? A bloody Tardis?' I rubbed my face in frustration. I was tired all of a sudden. So tired. And I remembered the birds, the horror of the dying birds and the fire in the sky glaring down at me through the waters of the lake, and I felt a sense of dread.

I contemplated ignoring The Door and simply going upstairs to bed to listen to some soothing music. I could have another brandy and a hot bath, and then, surely, nothing would keep me awake. But then the cat's neat little ying and yang head with its one white ear and one black ear appeared around the door and miaowed at me.

'Ok, ok, I'm coming!' I knocked back the last of the brandy for Dutch courage then set off reluctantly towards The Door.

I was in the sky, high above an extraordinary city made of white, shining buildings dotted about with vivid greens of parks and gardens. I wasn't floating or flying, alas, but found myself on one of an intricate series of delicate white bridges that was spanning the sky in all directions with no visible means of support. I was impossibly high up but felt no sense of vertigo. The view was breathtaking.

The cat was ahead of me, but every now and then it stopped and turned to make sure I was following. I tried to keep up, but was constantly drawn to the walls on either side of the bridge, leaning over to peer down at the city far below, alive with the purposeful movement of distant people, as tiny as ants.

At the end of each bridge I followed the cat onto the next. I tried to make sense of the order or direction of them but found none. Some bridges ran parallel with each other, others dissected or crossed, some didn't end at all but split into three new bridges, some – I soon discovered – appeared to go around in circles. I lost all sense of time. The cat trotted ahead of me throughout it all. I tried to catch up with it. I even tried asking it questions, but it just looked at me and blinked with feline inscrutability or washed itself briskly for a second before starting off again.

Bridge

after

bridge

after

bridge

after

bridge.

I grew weary of the view below me. The brightness of it began to hurt my eyes, and the motion of the people below became manic and indiscriminate. The muscles of my legs were tiring and a headache was starting to knot itself behind my forehead.

'Please, puss, stop!' I forced myself into a light jog in my attempt to catch up with the cat, but it just increased its own pace so that it could maintain its distance. At the end of the bridge, however, it stopped and watched me. Panting, I neared the end of the bridge then recognised something about it, a pair of white marble posts at the end of the balustrades.

'We've been here before!' I screamed at the cat who was still watching me through half-open eyes. 'Why are you doing this to me?'

The cat started to wash its paw.

'Argh!' I slid down the wall at the side of the bridge and lowered my head onto my knees in exhaustion and defeat. What could I do? How could I get out of this place? Where was Nella? Without any conscious effort on my part my mind wandered to a day many years before.

It had been my birthday. I had come home from work and Nella and Tom had made me put a blindfold on. Then they had taken my hands, one each, and led me through the house. 'Trust us, do you trust us?' Nella had said.

I let them lead me, compliantly and clumsily, until I felt a breeze blow over my face and realised I must be in the garden. Someone gently took the blindfold off me and Nella whispered for me to open my eyes.

'SURPRISE!'

The garden was full of fairy lights and candles, and trestle tables were out, laden with drinks and food. About thirty smiling faces stared back at me, family, friends, Sophie back from university. It was one of the nicest days of my life.

I came out of the memory, opened my eyes and looked at the cat. It was lying down now, its head on its paws. I had an idea.

I got up, stood in the middle of the bridge and closed my eyes. I held out my hand. 'I'm here, Nella. Show me the way.'

I waited.

I breathed.

I tried to stay calm.

I tried to neither hope or despair.

And then I felt her hand slip into mine and grip it firmly. Keeping my eyes shut I let her lead me. I surrendered completely to her. I let my limbs be loose and my shoulders relax. I trusted her, I always had. She moved at a steady pace, and I followed happily after her, relishing the warmth of her skin against mine. The darkness behind my closed eyelids filled with ink spills and blooms of colour and the air smelled sweet.

Eventually she stopped and let go of my hand. For a moment I stood still, my eyes still closed and my heart beating hard, then I opened my eyes and there was The Door, the span of the bridge shrinking to meet its threshold. I turned around and saw the crazy jumble of bridges I had passed over behind me. They had now distilled, each joining into the single one I was standing on. The endless city still sparkled and vibrated below me, giving me a momentary feeling of profound loneliness. Nella was nowhere to be seen. I sighed and walked through The Door to find myself back in my own garden. There was a rustle in the bushes at the end of the garden, the glint of a feline eye.

'Here, puss, come on, puss.' I crouched down and peered into the shadows, but the cat had gone.

'Just me on my own again then,' I said, straightening up. The night pressed around me and I felt so tired that I could have curled up on the dew-damp lawn and fallen asleep there and then. I yawned and dragged myself up the stairs to my lonely bed.

8.
THE DOOR TO THE ICE ISLANDS

Once upon a time it was a man's birthday. There were lots of reasons why he was not inclined to celebrate it. One of them was that he was exhausted. Another was that he was at that stage of life where every birthday reminded him that there was now less of his life left ahead than there was left behind. But more than anything, the idea of celebrating grated on his soul, because he had lost one of the people he loved most in the world and the idea of celebrating felt, at worst, like a betrayal; at best, like something he wasn't sure he had the strength to endure.

He had been sitting in his study for a while now, and had found his mind wandering to his mother. She had been dead for thirty years but at that moment he felt the presence of her, the memory of her, pressing against his back as if she were standing behind him.

He remembered how she would tell the story of his birth; that he had come early and unexpectedly during a holiday in Dorset; about the mad rush in his parent's old Renault to get to the hospital in time; to his inauspicious delivery in a village pub a few miles from Dorchester.

He hadn't thought of his mother in years but suddenly he missed her, with the passion and white-hot fear of a little boy who has got lost in a department store and thinks he'll never be found again. *Where is she*, he found himself thinking. *Had she simply ceased to be, or would she be waiting for him, with his wife, on the day he himself died?*

He realised at that moment that inside him was everyone he had ever been, layer upon layer, like a Russian doll. Inside him, somewhere, was the young man who had lost his mother just days after his first wedding; somewhere inside him was the little boy who had watched his father stamp his foot down onto a dying fledgling; inside him was the man now, struggling with the fact that he was one more year into late middle age and still in pain from the open wound of his grief.

He felt the journey of his life roll out behind him and it filled him with heartsick nostalgia. *Has every thread of my existence really led to this, just this?* he thought with despair. *Did every thread start just to lead to the deaths of those I love, to the mistakes I seem powerless to have stopped myself making?*

There was the rub at the heart of it all: Did I make the threads or did the threads make me?

...

'Stop being such a miserable old bastard, Dad. We're coming, and there's nothing you can do about it.'

'You're not getting out of it!' I heard Trisha say in the background. She must have been the one driving.

'Listen, Tom, I'm just not sure I'm up to it.'

'So, you're not up to having a nice laidback dinner with your family to celebrate your birthday, but you are up to sitting around feeling miserable all by yourself?'

I held the phone away from me and sighed. 'Ok, ok,' I brought it back to my ear again, 'you win. I'll have a shower and wash the miserable old bastard away until all that's left is the grumpy old git you know and love.'

I heard Tom laugh. 'That's the spirit, Dad. We won't be there till sevenish because Sophie's at work, so you've plenty of time. Why don't you have a nap or something?'

'A nap!' I replied, chagrined. 'I'm not eighty you know!'

'Ha ha, aren't you? I'd better go and change the card I got then.'

'Very funny.'

'Are you ok for wine?'

'I've got a couple of bottles of red, so maybe get a nice white or two.'

'Will do.'

'See you later.'

'Yep, see you later.'

I hung up the call and threw the phone on the bed. 'Come on, you old git,' I said out loud to myself. 'You're just going to have to get on with it.'

I showered and shaved and changed into a clean shirt and some reasonably smart chinos. After I'd laced my shoes at Nella's dressing table I stood and turned, and there was The Door.

'Oh God not now, please not now.'

I looked at The Door.

The Door did nothing.

I paced the room and tried not to look at The Door.

The Door stayed right where it was.

'Fuck it!'

I went to The Door and flung it open. An icy breeze hit me full in the face, the shock of it stopping the breath in my chest. I went to the wardrobe and pulled out a sweater, gloves and a woolly hat from my winter drawer and put them on.

'Ok, let's see what you've got for me this time.' I opened the door, but it was so bright on the other side that at first I couldn't see what was beyond it. I blinked several times and then shielded my eyes with the flat of my hand until eventually my eyes were able to make sense of the scene in front of me.

It was my own bedroom, made entirely of ice. Bed, dressing table, walls, doors, everything shone with a translucent brilliance. Through the window I could see what looked like open ocean, as if the room was on an island. The sky was pale blue and the sea, mirror still. The horizon was dotted by the outlines of other small islands and occasionally a seabird scythed through the freezing air, its cry faint and melancholic.

I was about to step over the threshold but something stopped me. With my hand still on the handle I turned back towards the room behind me and felt the warmth of the summer evening on my face. The colours of my bedroom were deep and warm. I turned back to the eye-watering brilliance of the room and cried out. Nella sat on the bed, looking ahead, her face peaceful.

'Nella, darling Nella.'

She turned to me and smiled. Then she stood up and walked towards the opposite wall. With a lurch in my stomach I saw that The Door was also on the other side of the room. Like everything else, this was a door made of ice.

She reached for the handle.

'No, Nella, please no, wait –'

She turned to me again. She looked sad. Impossibly and profoundly sad. A sob caught in my throat.

'Don't go, darling don't go! Let me hold you, one last time, just one last time!'

Nella turned away from me again and her hand closed around the handle and turned it. Nella's door opened letting in a gush of freezing air. It played over everything in the room making it shiver with movement and setting off a tinkling wave of sound.

I ran across the room after her, but by the time I'd reached the ice door she was gone and it had closed behind her.

'NELLA!'

Her name poured out of the primal depths of me like a howl. A terrible anguish came over me. I grabbed hold of the handle but it was so cold that I felt my skin burn and my fingers ache. I let go with a shout of pain.

My whole body shaking with cold I heard in the distance the pleasant rumble of voices and the high screech of Ella's laughter. The sound was coming from my bedroom and through The Door. I could hear a dog barking, someone mowing their lawn and a burst of birdsong.

My hand hovered over the ice handle. If I truly loved her I would go through it, I told myself. But another voice, small but insistent, told me that I knew that wasn't true.

'Granddad!' Ella's voice sounded closer now. I went back to The Door and peeked through.

I saw our bedroom, the patterned duvet still flung half off the bed, the door that should have been there also ajar letting in a wedge of yellowy light.

I swayed forward and back from my heels to the balls of my feet between the ice world and my own. My heart beat in my chest and I felt life flow through the crack in the door and throw itself over me like a warm blanket. It would be so easy to give in to that warmth, to step over the threshold. But that would mean never seeing Nella again, never holding her or talking to her. How could I bear that after only just finding her again?

Sophie's clear voice shot up the stairs. 'Come on, birthday boy, dinner's ready!'

EPILOGUE

Once upon a time a man packs boxes in an empty bedroom. He fills the last one, tapes it up and writes on it with a marker pen. He straightens up with a groan and looks about him. The dim light of dusk is coming through the window and the distant song of a blackbird makes the room nostalgic in its emptiness.

The man seems transfixed by the bare wall in front of him. There are the shadows of picture frames on the wall, but between them the gap is featureless and blank.

As if acting on an impulse the man goes over to the wall, takes the cap off the marker and, starting from the skirting board and working up, draws the outline of a life-sized door on the wall. Just an ordinary door, with a simple beaded detail and a round doorknob. He stands back and clasps his hands together as if he is praying, though he is not a religious man.

He watches the door.

Nothing happens.

His breath is coming quick and shallow.

Nothing happens.

'Oh Nella,' he says, with longing.

Nothing happens.

A sound comes from him, it could be a sob or it could be a stifled laugh. Only he knows which it is.

'Granddad!' The voice makes the man jump. It is soon followed by the sound of footsteps in the hall outside the room. A little girl comes in, her face red with exertion. 'I just carried a whole big box outside all by myself –' she stops and stares at the drawing of the door as if it is somehow familiar, then goes over and takes the man's hand. 'Time to go, Granddad.'

...

So there you have it. The answers to your questions, save one. Did he live happily ever after? Although that question is to be expected I have to say, it's not one I can truly answer. That's for John to decide.

SUPPORT IF YOU ARE GRIEVING

As I hope this story shows, there is no right or wrong way to grieve. Much has been done to help us understand grief, but the truth remains that each person's experience is unique.

If there is one truth within this, however, it is that you don't need to go through it alone. When I lost my father, just five months after the birth of my first son, I soon found out that I either needed to admit I needed help, or go under. As well as support from friends and family I went to my GP, who helped me access a grief counsellor on the NHS.

There are a myriad of charities and organisations that can help, some with specialisms such as support for people who have lost children or people who have lost a partner or sibling. Cruse Bereavement Care have a national network of trained bereavement volunteers to offer support to adults and children; The Good Grief Trust runs an annual 'Grief Awareness Week' and Marie Curie also has a comprehensive list that you can access from their website.

For links and more information please visit my website.
www.corinnaedwards-colledge.co.uk

Also by
Corinna Edwards-Colledge

Novels:
THE SOUL ROOM
RETURN OF THE MORRIGAN
ARGEMOURT

Novellas:
THE CALL

ABOUT THE AUTHOR

Corinna Edwards-Colledge was born and brought up in Chorlton-cum-Hardy in Manchester. She spent many happy childhood Kendal-mint-cake-fuelled hours exploring magical local sites like Alderley Edge and Styal Woods, and has taken an enduring love of the natural world into her writing.

She studied English and Media at the University of Sussex and went on to a diverse working life including time as a journalist and treading the boards in a play by Brian Behan. She now splits her time between being a union Branch Secretary and writing.

She has written three novels and two novellas and also writes poems and short stories. She lives in Brighton with her family and enjoys hot curries, cold white wine, long walks, passionate conversations and laughing until it hurts. Most of all she loves words, the infinite worlds they create and the limitless opportunities they provide to communicate and connect.

To keep in touch and hear about events, offers, new releases and to access a musical playlist to accompany The Door That Shouldn't Have Been There, visit **www.corinnaedwards-colledge.co.uk**
or connect on Facebook **@CorinnaAuthor**
and Instagram **@MrsMush**

ABOUT THE ILLUSTRATOR

Becky Gough is a visual artist living in Sussex with a background in Fine Art.

The sourcing, assembling and combination of imagery and forms provides the core of her practice in 2D collage, illustration, moving image, and mixed media work. She is concerned with themes of history and memory, oblivion, forgetting and the passing of time. Her work explores and manipulates found imagery from forgotten boxes in attics, second hand bookshops, diaries, postcards, photographs and the recesses of digital archives, drawing out the human presences that 'haunt' these materials.

In her work, you may encounter the faces, thoughts and imagery of those who might be lost and forgotten to time and history, a tribute to the many anonymous lives that may now exist out of lived memory, but linger on as fragments and residues in the material of the archive, the book and the photo album.

Collaborating with Corinna on *The Door That Shouldn't Have Been There* has been a wonderful exploration into their shared fascination with the traces of lives lived and past experiences as well as the phenomena of time, memory, and the desire to hold onto it.

You can see more of her art on her Instagram **@beckygoughcollage**

GREAT STORYTELLING DOESN'T JUST ENTERTAIN, IT ENERGISES

Claret Press' mission is simple: we publish engrossing books which engage with the issues of the day.
So we publish across a range of genres, both fiction and nonfiction. From award-winning page-turners to eye-opening travelogues, from captivating historical fiction to insightful memoirs, there's a Claret Press book for you.

To keep up to date about the going-ons at Claret Press, including book launches, zoom talks and other events, sign up to our newsletter through our website at **www.claretpress.com**.

You can also find us through Instagram **@claretpress** Twitter **@ClaretPress** and YouTube **@claretpress**